The Prince of Owr

The Prince of Owr

An Allegory for the Bride of Christ

Nancy Fowler Christenson

Ogden Fish Publishing

ISBN 978-1-9990781-0-2

Dedication

This little book was first dedicated
to the Grades 7, 8, and 9 girls
at Mamawi Atosketan Native School.
Each one of you is a princess.

Its re-release in 2019 comes with
a prayer for the boys at this school as well:
May each of you, through Christ,
find the prince inside yourself.

*Giving thanks to the Father,
who has qualified us to share
in the inheritance of the saints
in the kingdom of light.*

—Colossians 1:12, NASB & NIV

Table of Contents

The Prince of Owr

𝕭ridegroom in 𝖂aiting

Many, many years ago in the kingdom called Owr, there lived a handsome prince. His features were as noble and as pleasing as the chiselled work of the finest sculptor, and every maiden in the land sighed and swooned at the sight of his comely countenance and muscular stature. But his beauty was in much more than his form: it was in his eyes. Wise beyond his years they were, clear and deep like a woodland pool, and full of kindness, for this was his nature. Neither arrogant nor puffed up with pride in his father's power and riches, he was altogether approachable, whether to the court's highest official or the lowliest peasant in the land.

People said that he had his father's eyes, and this was a compliment indeed, because his father was much beloved of all his subjects. Not that the king was a liberal man—far from it. He had a rigorous standard of righteousness and a stringent sense of justice. Some, at first glance, thought him harsh. But it never took much musing to understand that this exacting standard was the very reflection of his love and concern for the well-being of his people.

The prince was of marriageable age—had been for a number of years, and this was, of course, one of the things that made the ladies flutter their eyelashes and drop their curtsies at his appearing. Any of them would have been thrilled to have his attentions rest on her, for even a moment.

But the prince's heart was not to be easily satisfied. He held the estate of marriage in reverence, and he would not lightly settle on just any beautiful bride. She had to be perfect—at least perfect for him, and he believed that he would recognize her when he saw her; he was sure that his heart would know her at first sight. Meanwhile he would not toy with such things. "Awaken not love until it pleases," was the way he put it.

On a day in spring when winter was fast fleeing, the prince decided to go for a long ride. He had been training a favourite colt—he had a way with animals—and today seemed a good day to take this green mount out in the sun for a new lesson: it was time to accustom the young horse to the weight and the clatter of the prince's armour. So it was that on this fine sunny day, coming through the woods on the homeward leg of his ride, only a few miles from the palace, he was in full armour with helmet and visor, only his eyes visible, and those only barely.

The snows and rains were over and gone for another year; the flowers had appeared, and the forest had the fresh beauty and the hope of promise that comes with every spring. It was in this setting that he happened upon a beautiful young woman— he quite startled her, really—he could tell by the expression on her face as she looked up. She was kneeling in the soft moss gathering tiny, perfect, purple crocuses, and she seemed to be suspended in time for a moment, with a wide-eyed look of surprise, lips parted, royal blossoms trailing from her poor, rough hands. He could see from her simple clothing that she was among the lowliest of the peasants in the land, but her beauty riveted him.

His heart was suddenly beating wildly beneath his breastplate, echoing in his ears. He knew he should say hello, but no word came to his lips. Usually an easy conversationalist in any company, he was struck dumb with shyness. He felt his face flushing hot behind his visor, and he was glad that she could not see the flustered awkwardness that had caught him so off-guard. He raised his gloved hand in greeting, bowed low in the saddle, and then gave the colt his heels.

As he manoeuvred the animal through the trees at a brisk trot, trying to shake off his embarrassment, he was no longer aware of the fresh mystique of the awakening forest around him. There was another beauty lodged front and centre in his mind, and he carried that pretty picture away with him toward home.

What a lovely face! What a gentle demeanour! But there was something else, something that threw a shadow on the image in his mind. What was it that he had seen in those eyes? It was a darkness of pain, or of dread, or of fear. He sighed. What a wonderful enigma!

In spite of himself, he felt his heart reaching back into the forest, seeking the maid, even as he turned his colt over to the grooms and went to wash for dinner. "O girl," he whispered under his breath, "you have stolen my heart with just one glance."

He said little at the meal. He was wondering what he could ever say to his father about a girl like this. Regardless of the drawing away of his heart, his mind did not see any sense in this attraction; no hope in its fulfillment. She was of such low estate.

He needed a confidante. Yes, as soon as he could reasonably excuse himself from dinner, he would seek out Kletos.

Kletos was an old and trusted servant of the king. He had been Jehonathan's tutor in a younger day, and he had been much more than that. In the times when the king was far a-field with war or business, Kletos had been a mentor and a friend. He still was.

Kletos listened quietly, watching his young master's face with fascination. Never had he seen the lively eyes so animated. This was something new.

"Yes," he said as the younger finished his story and posed a query, "yes, I will try to find out who she is. I will sit in the village inn over the next few evenings and listen to the old biddies and their husbands as they muse and gossip over their ale. I am no stranger there, and I will be discreet. No one will suspect a thing."

The news, when it came back to Jehonathan, was not welcome.

"She's already married," old Kletos told him gently. "Her name is Beulah, and she is the wife of a brutish man. Handsome, but brutish. I don't believe she has a happy life. But there you have it."

Jehonathan felt the new and wild hope in his heart go silent. So that was the way it was. He must have been mistaken about his feeling. This could not be the woman for him. He must honour her marriage. But was marriage still honourable if it was unhappy, maybe even cruel? It was a hard question, too hard for him. And it was too tender a thing to talk about right now, even with Kletos.

As for a wife, he would have to go back to hoping for that which, for now, had no substance for him. He would wait, and he would keep his eyes open.

Defeating the Enemy

Spring matured into summer. Jehonathan felt that he was always waiting and watching, and in his heart he realized that he was not really looking for a new love. Without meaning to, and feeling rather guilty for it, he found himself ever watching, as he rode through the woods or the village, for *her*. For Beulah. He yearned to see her, to admire her, even from a distance.

He never even glimpsed her, though, until the day of the Harvest Festival. It was a grand occasion, beginning with a royal parade at high noon. The peasant farmers and shepherds always came from miles around and joined the trades-folk and other townspeople for a day of celebration and games, feasting and revelry.

The king led the parade as always, followed by his officers and the whole army, all in full armour. Bringing up the rearguard was the crown prince, Jehonathan, on his high-stepping colt, flanked by his aides.

The sun beat down on his shining armour, and he could feel the sweat beading and trickling down his face under the visor. The heat was almost overwhelming. Still, it was a glorious day, and he felt full and exhilarated as he waved back to his people. Excitement rang in the air. The Harvest Festival was always the highlight of the long summer.

Jehonathan knew that inevitably some the peasants would get carried away with their revelry. *Never mind the peasants,* he thought wryly, *some of the noblemen will too, before the end of the day!* It was not his style, but he had learned to follow the lead of his father: "Live and let live"—so long as it was harmless.

The colt moved easily underneath him, neck arched, bobbing its head, seemingly keeping time with the creak of leather and rattle of armour. There had been a light rain during the night, settling the dust on the street and cleaning it from the air. It had been so clear earlier when he'd gone down to the stable, just after the sun was up, that even the distant mountains seemed closer.

Days like this reminded him of something his father sometimes quoted—something that the ancients had written about the reign of a righteous king. He let it roll through his mind again, the movement of the horse and the hum of the crowd lulling him deep inside his thoughts: *And he shall be as the light of the morning, when the sun riseth, even a morning without clouds; as the tender grass springing out of the earth by clear shining after rain.* He didn't quite understand the symbolism, but it made his heart swell with earnestness. *When I become king,* he thought, *I want to be that kind of ruler.*

In the milling crowds off to his left, he was suddenly aware of a skirmish of action. He snapped out of his reverie, and as he riveted his gaze there, he was surprised to see the pretty face that had so haunted his dreams, both waking and sleeping.

But what was this? Her face was distraught, and she was being roughly and crudely handled by a strapping young lout. He evidently had already imbibed far too much liquor, as had his companions, and even as the choler rose in Jehonathan's being, he saw the young woman shoved and pawed and fondled among the whole group of them, their raucous laughter rising above the noise of the crowd.

The prince's head pounded with rage, and his heart exploded with grief. He responded from his gut, without thought or reason. He wrested his lance from its scabbard and spurred the colt into the crowd, which parted in a panic before him. Within seconds he was upon the group of them. His lance found its mark, running through the vitals of the ringleader of this vile game. The other men fled into the crowd, losing themselves quickly in the confusion, even as Jehonathan came vaulting off his horse. He planted a boot on the side of the villain's head, right next to a staring eye that was fast glazing over, and he cried out to the crowd:

"No one, no one in my father's kingdom will humiliate or violate a woman and live to tell about it! The strength of a man, the glory of a man, is to honour and protect a woman!" He withdrew the bloodied lance and held it high over his head for emphasis. "In the name of the King!" he shouted.

He ground the heel of his boot down hard on that hateful face, now a mask of death, crushing it into the dirt so violently that it made his heel throb. Then he turned and leapt back onto his horse. The whole thing had taken hardly a minute.

He was now in a sudden confusion of self-consciousness. People were staring. He was aware of some older women comforting the young peasant girl, lifting her from the dust where she had been shoved in the men's haste. For a moment she met his gaze. He saw in her eyes a strange mixture of grief and gratitude. Once again he was glad for his visor, glad that she could not see him face to face.

He couldn't stay here. And he couldn't join back into the parade. He spun the colt, turning his back on the whole scene, and headed out of the village at a hard gallop.

He would spend the rest of the day alone at the palace. He wouldn't really be missed. The celebration would continue on. A skirmish like this one on such a wild day was like dropping a large millstone in a pond—a big splash, but within moments, no sign of anything having happened.

His own heart was not calming quite so easily. Was that the young woman's husband that he just butchered? He couldn't find it in himself to be sorry, but he wondered how she was taking it. He would have to employ Kletos's eyes and ears again, once the festival was over and life was back to normal.

And something else—if her husband was dead, she would likely have difficulty supporting herself. Well, Kletos would help him think of something.

A Loving Conspiracy

She sells a variety of wares in the market," Kletos was telling him.

"Then go there tomorrow and buy everything she has," Jehonathan cried impetuously, pulling a bag of gold coins from his bosom, "and just give it all away to someone, somewhere—anyone, anywhere!"

"Now, now," said the old tutor, "no need for that. Better a day-by-day provision than a sudden windfall. Besides, many of her things would be useful in the palace on an ongoing basis. Let her keep busy, and let her keep what dignity she has. I will go there every few days and keep her commerce prospering. She will grow comfortable with me. Perhaps I can even become a confidante and a comfort to her. She needs a friend."

"How I would love to be that friend!" Jehonathan sighed longingly. "But for now it is expedient that I stay away."

The older man nodded his agreement. "'To everything there is a season,'" he quoted. "Be patient. Your time will come. At least you can rest in knowing that you have arranged for her provision, her protection, and her comfort."

The Prince of Owr

It was spring again, and there came a day when the king drew his son aside for a heart-to-heart talk. Jehonathan was not surprised when his father brought up the subject of marriage.

"I am getting on in years," the elder said, "and it is soon time that I give you my crown. Yours will be the kingdom and the power and the glory. But first you should have a wife. A virtuous woman is a gift from Providence, and her value is above many precious gems. You are a wise son, but a good maid will make you wiser. She will temper your character and sharpen the iron of your wisdom, your wit, and your compassion."

"Alas, my father, I would take a wife, but I love a woman already, of whom I fear you will disapprove. She is of low estate, a simple peasant; furthermore, she is not a maiden but a widow. I cannot tell you why I love her so; I only know that I do."

"My son, where did you get the idea that I would not approve of such a woman? There is no dishonour in being poor. I love all of my subjects, and some of the finest characters I know have neither lands nor goods. The poor will always be with us, and they are often wealthy in ways by which we, too, could be enriched.

"As for her having been married and widowed, there is no shame in having loved and lost, though often that weight is found to lie heavy on such a woman's heart. You have my ready blessing. I will love any woman that you set your heart upon. So, my son, what prevents you? Rise up and make your desire known."

"O Father," Jehonathan replied, "there is something further that hinders me, and something much more difficult to solve.

My eyes have met the come-hither gaze of a hundred young ladies, some of them shameless, and not one of them has ever known me for who I am. They are enamoured by my visage, and they desire me for my father's wealth and power. They covet the prestige, the position, and the security for the future that my station in life promises.

"But I want a woman who will regard neither my stature nor my countenance; a woman who, rather, will look upon my heart. I yearn to be known, really known, and to be loved, simply for who I am. I don't mean to sound ungrateful; it is a privilege to have been born into royalty. It's an honour to serve my people, even now as the crown prince, and much more it will be to be king. But sometimes it seems a lonely calling, and I have longed for a companion who will willingly and lovingly yoke herself to me.

"Now I love this peasant girl, and the conundrum is more complex still: not only might the lure of my riches draw this woman to marry me without love, so might her fear of insulting the future king by her refusal cause her to marry even if she might want to decline. How could I ever be sure of the sincerity of her love, even if she accepted mine?"

"You are a wise son," said the king affectionately, "and you make your father glad. You have spoken well, and your concerns are certainly not unfounded. We will send for Kletos to join his wisdom with ours: we need more now than we share between us. And speaking of whom, now there is an example of a fine fellow, however lowly his estate. He is only a peasant, but over the years he has become a valued advisor and a trusted friend, the best a man could ask for. You need not fear to woo a peasant for your bride. Gold is found in the commonest of ore."

It was a wonderful plan the three of them forged in the king's library that night. The prince would lay aside his glory for a time and take upon himself the garb of a humble shepherd, tending some of the king's flocks. It was a natural choice for a disguise: of all the varied experiences that Kletos had seen fit to include in the young prince's education, tending the sheep had been one of the younger's favourites, and so he was not in any sense ignorant of this vocation. Some peasant's clothing, and Jehonathan could jump in like a duck into water.

The king's pastures bordered the woods where the young woman lived, alone now in the place that had been her husband's, a little cottage not far from where Jehonathan had first seen her. Days she spent at the market, selling her wares, but early and in the evening she was known to often walk in the woods and through the meadow. The prince could approach her there, in her own world in more ways than one. How glad he was that she had never laid eyes on his face. She would not know him for who he really was, the crown prince, and he would not reveal that until the proper time. Meanwhile she would get to know the real Jehonathan.

The three men bade each other goodnight, well pleased with their idea. Kletos paused in the hallway with his old hat in his hands. "There is an ancient poem," he said, "and at the moment the name of the writer escapes me. But there is a line therein that speaks of 'lifting the meek from the dust and placing them among princes.' Tonight those words are ringing in my heart as though they have been shouted from the very heavens."

Winning Her Trust

The first time Jehonathan saw her, he as a shepherd, she was walking barefoot in the meadow very early in the morning. She was unaware of eyes upon her, unselfconscious and carefree. He watched her as she gathered wildflowers, plucking them and laying them in a shallow basket.

As the sun was coming up over the faraway mountains, she reached up and pulled the pins from her hair. The long plaits fell down over her shoulders, slowly unweaving themselves. She shook her head a little, and the tresses fell loose, highlights reflecting in the early, slanted rays.

His breath caught in his throat: he thought that he had never seen anything so lovely. As she came closer, he, not wanting to be caught spying in secret, called a greeting to her from under the apple tree where he sat. A sweet voice echoed his salutation. She waved a hand and walked on.

That was how their friendship began, and it moved ahead very slowly. He felt that he had to be careful, as though she might be frightened if he reached out to her too quickly. She reminded him of a deer grazing among the lilies: lovely and graceful, but cautious and tentative. Very much on the alert.

Easily startled. Quick to move along and slip out of sight again among the trees.

Finally one day he invited her to sit and talk awhile under his tree, and she assented, gathering her faded skirts about her carefully so that just her pretty little feet showed as she sat in the grass. She wrapped her arms around her knees, turning her face toward him now and then as they talked. Her hair, loose again this morning, slid back and forth across her back with the movement of her head, shining in the sun.

He felt like a banquet was laid out before him, such a feast it was to his eyes to have her so near. Her eyes were gentle, and a bit sad, like dove's eyes. Her skin was brown from the sun, unlike the fine ladies of the court. Those women had their own kind of beauty, but this girl—oh, she was like a lily among thorns. She was lithe and strong for a woman, yet so utterly feminine. And her voice, when she spoke, was so like a caress that it made his head spin.

A quotation from a poem ran through his mind. He savoured the words. They might have been his own, so perfectly did they fit the moment.

> *Oh, let me see your form*
> *And let me hear your voice*
> *For your voice is sweet*
> *And your form is lovely*

He longed to speak the words aloud, but it was far too soon. *To everything there is a season, and a time to every purpose under the heaven,* the same poet had said, *a time to keep silence and a time to speak.* Aloud, he spoke only of general things—

the weather, the sheep, her craft—speaking easily and softly, sensing that time, and lots of it, would work in his favour.

After that, she came to the meadow frequently, and each time, she readily joined him under the tree. They talked by the hour, and although Jehonathan couldn't be sure, he thought she was comfortable with him and happy to be there.

The day finally came when he told her how beautiful she was, and that he had been in love with her for a long time. He didn't tell her that she had stolen his heart long before she ever met him face to face. He had loved her from a distance; delivered her from her cruel husband—anonymously. He had provided for her and watched over her without her ever suspecting. Someday she would come to understand all this. But for now he simply declared his love and admiration.

He could see by the warmth in her eyes that she was glad for his admission, but there was a shadow there as well. Never mind—he would proceed.

"Beulah, fair maiden, I want you to be my wife," he said longingly.

The shadow darkened. "I am not a maid," she answered. "I have had a husband, and now I am a widow."

"I'm sorry," he ventured. "What happened to him?" He felt just a little bit deceitful, pretending to know nothing of a matter about which he had first-hand knowledge.

"It was a fray at the annual festival," she said, "last year. He was drunken and disorderly. His conduct displeased the king's royal guard, and one of them ran him through with his sword."

"I'm sorry," he said again, and once more he felt that he was being duplicitous. He didn't feel sorry at all that the man was dead, much less that it was by his own hand. Any man who would treat a woman like that, especially a precious girl like this—well, it still made his blood boil. And yet the death of that knave had caused this dear one grief, and probably considerable anxiety for the future as well, leaving her to live off her own meagre commerce and the kindnesses of other people.

After a short silence, he ventured to question her further. He would withdraw his probing at once should he sense her pulling back. "Was it a happy marriage?" he asked gently, even though he had heard otherwise.

She frowned and hesitated, seeming to search for the right words. "He was a hard man," she answered finally, simply.

"Then why did you marry him?" he asked.

"It's a long story," she said.

Jehonathan got to his feet and surveyed the pasture. All was peaceful, the sheep placidly grazing. He settled himself once more against the trunk of the tree. "I've got all the time in the world," he said.

Touching Her Wounds

He could see in her face, as she began to talk, that she trusted him. It was good that he had not hurried his friendship with her. She spoke slowly at first, cautiously, but she seemed to gain courage as she spoke.

"I was young and very naive," she said, "and I happened to catch his eye. He gave me a lot of attention, and he charmed me with his words. I was carried away by his flattery. I knew that he desired me: even though I didn't really understand it at my age, I felt it. It made me feel so special, so valuable. I was loved by a man!

"Then one day he took me for a walk in the woods. I suppose I was foolish to go so far alone, away from the safety of the village, but I didn't understand the way of a man with a maid. He forced himself upon me, there in the forest. I was so ashamed for the loss of my virtue, and I was embarrassed that I had been so stupid. I have never told anyone what happened that day.

"Afterwards, he said he wanted to marry me. I was afraid of him now, but who else would want me? I feared more being left alone, with no provision and nobody to be with for my whole life. Surely it would be best to marry, I thought.

"But I didn't know that he would become so cruel. He often made sport of me with his friends, as though I were a harlot. And when he desired me, he seemed like an animal, and that made me feel no better than an animal myself.

"What drew me to him in the beginning was his desire for me. He made me feel loved. How I wish that he had honoured me more than he desired me, because now I understand that honour is a higher form of love than is desire. Any animal can desire. But only a good man has honour—and can bestow honour."

Beulah's voice trailed off in wistfulness, and she sat with her eyes downcast, pretending to study a daisy that she held in her hand. Tears trickled down her cheeks, but she seemed unaware of them. She carefully began to pluck petals from the daisy.

Jehonathan was silent for a long while. That is, he did not speak aloud, but his heart and mind roared with conflicting thoughts and emotions. He felt tears forming in his own eyes. He stared hard at the mountains, willing himself not to blink. The tears must dry there in his eyes. He would not let them spill.

"I hate that dog for what he did to you," he said bitterly. "What a wicked, despicable excuse for a man! I hate him!"

Now her eyes met his. "Perhaps you should not be so hard on him," she said. "Maybe he's not the only wicked one."

"What do you mean by that?"

She looked away again and bit her lip as the tears coursed down her cheeks once more. Again she looked at him, then away. "I feel like I can tell you anything," she said softly. She said it like a statement, but it seemed to leave a question hanging in the air.

"You can," he said earnestly. "You can tell me anything."

"Oh, please don't despise me," she pleaded suddenly.

"Never," he said.

"There are things in my own heart that frighten me almost more than he did," she began. "In spite of what I've told you, the truth is that I wanted him to desire me. Somehow I even wanted him to use me. And even when he and his friends made a game of my body, part of me revelled in it. I think I just wanted so much to be wanted. Afterwards I would be overcome with a sick feeling, like pleasure and pain all mixed in together. I don't know why I was like that, but there must be something very wicked in me. I think I must have deserved everything that happened to me. I think I really must be a very bad person."

She fell silent at last. The tears had stopped. In their place was an awful stillness, like the stillness of death.

Silence hung between them. Jehonathan thought of many things he might say, but none of them seemed quite right. All the thoughts kept rolling back into one thought, a thought that undergirded every other thing in his heart. He spoke it aloud, for the second time that day: "I love you, Beulah, and I want you to be my wife."

She leapt to her feet and ran across the meadow, disappearing into the woods.

His heart was breaking, but he sat there and let her go. *Perhaps it's best if she's alone right now,* he thought. *I will see her tomorrow.* Her visits with him under the apple tree had become almost a daily occurrence, giving him confidence over the weeks that his feelings were reciprocated and her trust was growing. And so he was sure that the visits would continue.

But she did not come the next day, nor the next, neither the next one after that, and day by day a heaviness grew inside him, a fear that the intimate conversation had undone her and driven her back into hiding.

Healing Begins

A fortnight passed, during which he had much time for thought—too much time. The days dragged by, an agony of uncertainty and loneliness. Now another day had dawned, and although the weather was still holding fine, there was the threat of a storm hanging over the mountains. The sheep were restless, and their uneasiness accentuated Jehonathan's moodiness all the more.

As the afternoon drew on, so did the dark clouds, heavy and ominous. Amid the rumbling crescendo of approaching thunder, Jehonathan heard another sound—frantic bleating of sheep. Shaking off his melancholy reverie, he leapt to his feet and ran in the direction of the distress. A wolf had a young lamb and was mauling it, dragging it away from the flock. With sudden anger and a reckless courage fuelled by his unhappiness, he was upon the beast in a moment, flogging it with his staff and driving it away before it could do more damage.

Tenderly, he wrapped the frightened little thing in his cloak and carried it back to the tree to examine the wounds more carefully. It looked to be in bad shape, but Jehonathan was sure that it could be saved. He would cut the day short and head back with the flock early. There were servants at the castle who would doctor it skillfully.

So engrossed was he that he failed to notice the approach of the fair figure of his dreams. She was almost upon him when he saw her. He sprang, surprised, to his feet and, for a moment forgetting his peasant persona, he gave a low, courtly bow.

At this formal gesture, her sombre countenance brightened and she almost smiled. But her voice, when she spoke, trembled.

"I couldn't stay away any longer," she began. "I feel I must ask your pardon for running away."

Jehonathan could see the tears springing up in her eyes already, and he knew that the past two weeks had seen as much or more torment for her than for him. In spite of his caution, he put his arms around her and drew her to him. He wanted to comfort her; he couldn't bear her distress any longer. She did not resist but rather let him hold her, laying her head carefully on his shoulder and shaking with suppressed sobs.

"I love you," he told her simply.

At this reassurance, the weeping came on in earnest. After a bit, it subsided, and she seemed to gather some resolve. She pushed back from him until she could look up into his face. "Thank you for loving me," she said. "For so long I have felt unlovable. But you deserve a much better woman than I."

He began to protest, but she went on: "I am so used and unclean," she said, her eyes welling up again. "I am ashamed for you to love me."

"It wasn't your fault that you were treated so," he countered. "What happened is no reflection on your virtue."

"But it *was* my fault," she said, the tears flowing once more. "I was foolish, and I was wicked. I don't know that I was ever virtuous."

"I love you," he said. "Let that be your virtue."

"I don't deserve you. You are so good that I feel all the more unworthy in comparison. I feel like I belong in a gutter somewhere."

He gazed at her. It was beyond him how one so beautiful could have such ugly feelings. "To me," he said, "you are a princess. I would lay down my life for you."

She dropped her eyes, unable to meet his gaze any longer.

"I've had much time to think about the things you told me," said Jehonathan. "Will you allow me to tell you what I have concluded?"

"Yes," she answered, "please do."

"The way you were treated by that man is the way you came to feel about yourself, and so that is what you became—or at least, what you thought you were. But I have set my love upon you. If you will accept my love—if you will choose to receive it, it will change the way you feel about yourself, and again that will determine what you become. I will not love you any more than I do now, for that is not possible. But you will be happier, and that will make me even happier than I am this day.

"Don't you see?" he said. "I love you completely, just the way you are, in spite of whatever has happened. And my love is big enough to cover it all, whether the wrongs you have done or the wrongs that have been committed against you.

"Anyway," he went on, "my father always says that the fullest life and greatest joy come not on a smooth path but on the rocky journey from woundedness into healing."

She was crying again, but there seemed to be a cleansing relief in the tears now. "What could I ever do to deserve this kind of love?" she questioned, half to herself.

Jehonathan knew that she did not expect a response, but he answered anyway: "I don't want you to try to earn my love," he said. "Please just receive it, a gift that I want to give to you."

Coming Home

The emotional exchange had been so intense that neither had noticed the advent of the storm. Now he saw that she was shivering in the sudden torrent of rain and the buffeting of the wind. Quickly he unwrapped his cloak from around the injured lamb and wrapped his precious Beulah in it, holding her close. It was then he noticed that it was stained with the blood of the lamb.

"I'm sorry," he began, showing her the soil, but she shook her head. "It's all right," she said. She paused a moment, thinking, and then her face lit up with a smile, as sudden and welcome as when the sun pops out from behind a dark cloud. "Do you know—it not just all right; I think it's quite wonderful."

"Oh?"

"The blood convinces me of your love."

"How do you mean?" he asked, thoroughly puzzled.

She started to laugh for sheer joy. It was the first time he had heard her laugh, and it was music to him.

"Oh, my dear, humble shepherd! That you would have such concern for a wounded little lamb…that you didn't even think about your cloak getting all bloody and ruined…well, now I know that my heart will be safe with you. I have felt like that lamb, terrorized by a mongrel dog, but I can feel the wounds beginning to heal, even now."

Jehonathan's heart sang. She was receiving his love, and he could already see that it was making her a brand-new person. "Will you come by here tomorrow," he asked, "provided that the weather clears up? I want to take you to meet my father. I will bring a friend to stay with the sheep."

She didn't answer; she seemed unable to speak now, but she nodded and her eyes shone with a light that dispelled all the shadows that had lingered there so long. Then she handed back his cloak and turned and ran gracefully away, disappearing into the rain and wind, seemingly oblivious now of the cold.

Jehonathan slowly wrapped the lamb in the cloak again, and then, carrying it in his bosom, he called the sheep. They knew his voice well by now, and they followed him obediently. The trek back to the palace yards was long enough in fair weather, never mind when the trail was mired in mud, but Jehonathan felt like he was walking on air all the way. *Finally!* he exulted in his heart, *I am my beloved's and she is mine!*

"I've brought my horse," he told her the next day, "because it's a long walk back to my father's."

"Wherever did you get such a fine horse?" she asked, her eyes still shining.

"My father gave him to me," he said. "I raised him from a foal." This was certainly true, and yet it did not give too much away too quickly. She would know the whole truth soon enough. "Every good thing I have," he went on, "my father has given me. And one day soon, everything he has will be mine. And all that is mine will be yours.”

He swung onto the horse then reached down and pulled her up behind him. “Come, my fair one,” he said, “let us be going. I want to show you the place that’s been prepared for you.”

The End

About the Story

The Inspiration

This story came about as a result of several events working as catalysts one with another. First: I was reading *The Sacred Romance* by Brent Curtis and John Eldredge when I came across something quoted from *Disappointment with God* (page 80) by Philip Yancey, who in turn was quoting Soren Kierkegaard.

Suppose there was a king who loved a humble maiden. The king was like no other king. Every statesman trembled before his power. No one dared breathe a word against him, for he had the strength to crush all opponents. And yet this mighty king was melted by love for a humble maiden. How could he declare his love for her? In an odd sort of way, his kingliness tied his hands. If he brought her to the palace and crowned her head with jewels and clothed her body in royal robes, she would surely not resist— no one dared resist him. But would she love him?

She would say she loved him, of course, but would she truly? Or would she live with him in fear, nursing a private grief for the life she had left behind? Would she be happy at his side? How could he know? If he rode to her forest cottage in his royal carriage with an armed escort waving bright banners, that too would overwhelm her. He did not want a cringing subject. He wanted a lover, an equal. He wanted her to forget that he was a king and she a humble maiden and to let shared love cross the gulf between them. For it is only in love that the unequal can be made equal.

Curtis and Eldredge go on then to summarize the resolution of Kierkegaard's analogy: "The king clothes himself as a beggar and renounces his throne in order to win her hand. The Incarnation, the life and the death of Jesus, answers once and for all the question, 'What is God's heart toward me?'"

What a beautiful picture of the love God has for us—and what an insight into Christ laying aside His glory and clothing Himself with our humanity. It illustrates so beautifully a great truth of the Incarnation: Christ shed His royal identity and disguised Himself in flesh so that He could meet us and woo us on our own "turf." It also portrays a side of the heart of God that I had not considered before: His desire—His need (if indeed God *can* need)—to be known and loved and submitted to for who He is—not for His rich resources and blessings, not for His fearsome authority and power—but simply and honestly for His person. It was a concept that begged to be developed—a yarn that longed to be spun: a story, not of a king, I decided, but of the son of a king, who chose to take for his bride one far beneath his status.

A second factor: I had been exposed a few months earlier to several different resources—notably *Wakening the Dead* by

John Eldredge and Lisa Bevere's *Kissed the Girls and Made Them Cry*, as well as Lisa's video seminar, *Purity's Power*—all of which make use of well-known fairy tales, in places, to draw out and illustrate spiritual truths. Metaphorical and allegorical writing is a form that comes naturally to me. I think that way and speak that way frequently. It helps me to grasp truth—and to pass it on. And so these three works, too, inspired me to write an allegorical fairy tale to portray the beauty and reality of these truths.

The third and most important catalyst to precipitate this project was this: I was asked to bring the video series on purity (above) into a school on the reserve nearby to do a weekly session with the Grades 7, 8, and 9 girls. This assignment-from-God (which is what it clearly was to me) filled me with both excitement and dread. The subject of women's purity is very dear to my heart, and I have longed for an opportunity to work effectively with teenage girls on these matters, but this door was opening onto a scene that was way, way out of my comfort zone. I don't know about the state of affairs on other First Nations reserves, but here, drug abuse and alcoholism are rampant, as are all forms of child abuse: neglect, emotional and physical abuse, and incest. Not surprisingly, suicide is an almost weekly occurrence, and its victims are frequently teenagers. Just recently there, a ten-year-old girl succeeded in taking her life.

I knew that some of the girls I would be working with would be very difficult kids, very disturbed, very wounded. (The positive side, though, was that the school was a Christian one, run by Seventh Day Adventists, so I would have complete freedom to speak from a biblical perspective, offer the hope of the gospel, and use prayer as needed.)

It was a frightening challenge. But it was while I was working through my reservations and apprehension that I began to feel God's heart toward these girls. Not only did He want to woo these girls, right where they live, He wanted them to know that there was nothing they had done or could ever do, nothing that had happened to them or could ever happen, that would prevent or diminish His love for them—nothing that disqualified them from His promise of happy-ever-after. He wanted to tell them that He sees each of them as a princess, however rough her disguise might be.

Therefore, I decided, not only would the prince in my story fall in love with a girl far below his high estate (as the king in Kierkegaard's scenario), she would be a terribly wounded girl who would be restored by the healing power of love. In this way I am endeavouring to speak hope into the hearts of the girls at Mamawi, and into the hearts of girls and women everywhere, because all of us are unwhole in one way or another. It's simply a fact of life in this fallen world in which we live.

God wants to woo and win the heart of every woman and girl with His unconditional, unfailing, healing love. And not just the "gentler" sex: the men and boys too. Here the analogy breaks down a little, for it may be difficult for men and boys to identify with Beulah. But so they should; so should we all, for men and boys as well as women and girls are all a part of the Bride of Christ. Sadly, every one of us has inadvertently fallen short of what God intended for us and so missed out on the fullness of His blessings. But every single one of us, God desires to win over and restore.

So this story, although it is dedicated specifically to the girls at Mamawi Atosketan Native School, is a fairy tale for the whole Bride of Christ, for "whomsoever might believe."

A Message Within the Message

But before I go on, let me say this: Within the spiritual symbolism of this story is a simpler message, written to the heart of every woman and girl. It's a call to believe once again in a dream that many a girl has not dared believe for a long time, a childhood fantasy—the hope that somewhere out there, there is a handsome and loving prince, just for her, who will recognize and perceive everything in her that is virtuous and beautiful—in spite of appearances—and who will forgive and cover over everything that is less than perfect or even wicked and ungodly.

Each one of us women who has found the Lord has found that heavenly Prince, the Lover of our soul. He sees each of us as His princess. But also, it is He who has placed in our heart the longing for an earthly prince, a lover who, though he himself is no more perfect than we, knows and thereby reflects the grace and unconditional love of God. I believe that God wants us as women to begin believing Him to fulfill that dream right here on earth.

It was interesting: my daughter Rachel (at this point fourteen years old) had a friend over and was telling her about this fairy tale I was working on. So I told the friend that it was initially a story for girls and women, and I explained some of the things I have said above, about portraying God's love for us, about restoring hope in an earthly prince, and then I said, "But it's also a story for men and boys." I was going to explain about males, too, being a part of what's called the Bride of Christ, but Rachel interjected:

"Yeah," she said, "'cause they need to find the prince inside themselves."

How very perceptive! Yes, I believe that God wants to inspire men and boys to rise to His standard, to teach each of them to love a woman more than he loves himself, to lay down his life for her, "honouring the woman as [physically] weaker" (1 Peter 3:7, AMPC). "Husbands," comes the exhortation in Ephesians, "love your wives, as Christ loved the church and gave Himself up for her" (5:25, AMPC).

But one caution, ladies: If you are terribly unhappy or even just quietly dissatisfied in your marriage, the message here is *not* that you go hoping for a new lover who will bump off your husband and sweep you off your feet. Your Prince is Jesus Christ the Righteous. Look to Him to slay the enemy, in the lives of both you and your husband. Your husband is not your problem (Ephesians 6:12); neither is a new husband your solution. If you put your trust in God—really, seeking Him with full obedience, He will make everything beautiful in *His* time (cf. Ecclesiastes 3:11). "He is a rewarder of them that diligently seek Him" (Hebrews 11:6).

A Very Unhappy Marriage

Back to the spiritual side of the story: Beulah, of course, represents the Bride of Christ. Her name (taken from Isaiah 62:4) means "married." Like her, we are (spiritually speaking) already married when our heavenly Prince comes into our lives. And to whom or what are we married—bound by and subject to—when we meet the true Lover of our soul? Different "husbands" for different people. Here are three examples:

> 1. Wickedness perpetrated on us by others, as well as our own questionable choices made "in ignorance and unbelief" (1 Timothy 1:13, NIV), which have left us bound to a painful past and/or a difficult present.

> 2. Our basic sin nature, inherited from Adam, which seems to continually drag us into doing what we know is wrong (cf. Romans 7:14-24).

> 3. Legalism, which feeds off our natural tendency to self-righteousness and drives us to try (though perhaps subconsciously) to please God by doing the right things.

These three examples are not exclusive categories: we may be the victim of two or more of these dynamics. They are basic ingredients for an unhappy life, and the mix is a little different for each person. And in every case, the devil will take whatever occasion he can to "stir the pot"—exacerbating our woundedness, increasing our temptations, and twisting the Word of God and using it as a big stick with which to flog us. He is the sinister mastermind behind it all; he is the enemy of our souls.

A Metaphor from Scripture

In Romans Chapter 7, Paul talks about another "first husband," one that is common to all of us, regardless of individual circumstances. He does so to illustrate a powerful spiritual concept. He begins by reminding us, in verses 1-3, that only by death can the marriage bond be legitimately and effectively severed. Then, using marriage as a metaphor, he presents these ideas in verse 4:

1. We all are, or were, married to the law.

2. We who believe on Christ died with Him on the Cross.

3. We are hence freed from our first marriage, free to marry again.

4. Our new husband is Christ.

So, Paul is saying, we start out married to the law—all of us—not just the Jews. Bear in mind that this letter of Paul's was written to the new Christians in Rome, the majority of whom, according to the notes in the KJV Study Bible, were Gentiles. Romans 2:15 tells us that even the Gentiles show "the work of the law written in their hearts, their conscience also bearing witness, and their thoughts the mean while accusing or else excusing one another" (KJV). In other words, inherent in the unbeliever's conscience, their basic knowledge of right and wrong, is God's law. This word for "law," the law that is written in all of our hearts, is the same Greek word as the one for the Jewish law and the same one that Romans 7 tells us we're "married" to.

Marriage usually brings forth children. It is no different here. Paul says that in our marriage to the law, we brought forth "fruit unto death" (v.5, KJV). (Fruit here is a biblical term for children, as in "fruit of the womb.") All of the children born of this marriage have brought sorrow and death into our lives. Why? Is the law bad? Certainly not, says Paul emphatically (cf. v.7). "The law is holy," says verse 12, KJV, "and the commandment holy, and just, and good."

But the law, though it was "intended to bring life" (v.10, AMPC), brought death, because it was "weak through the flesh" (Romans 8:3)—weak through *our* flesh. The paternity of the law brought out, one might say, a congenital weakness in us.

Here are the names of some of the "children" born of the union of the law and our flesh: Rebellion, Guilt, Insecurity, and two sets of fraternal twins—Shame and Pride, and Self-Loathing and Self-Justification. And although these "children" may be as different from one another as night from day (as children tend to be), make no doubt about it: their parentage is the same.

In our unhappy marriage with the law, the devil is the ever-present opportunist. One might even say that he was responsible for the original meeting of the "wife" (humanity) and the "husband" (the law). Let's go back to the Garden for a moment: Remember that it was the devil who introduced mankind to the knowledge of good and evil (a foreshadowing of the law), drawing them away from a loving, trusting relationship with God. This is how sin entered into the world, through Adam (Romans 5:12), granted, but by the enemy's devices.

Generations later, God gave the law to mankind through Moses—to make humanity accountable to His standard, to expose the sin nature for what it is, and to show us our need of a Saviour (Romans 7:13; Gal. 3:24). But our enemy uses the law for subversive purposes: to arouse sin in us; to taunt and tempt our flesh with what we are not supposed to do (Romans 3:20b, 7:7-8); and then, when we fail, to heap condemnation on us.

But we who believe are crucified with Christ (Romans 6:6) and so are freed from the law. We must understand this, so I'll say it again: Romans 7:4-6 explains, by the marriage metaphor, that our vicarious death in Christ has legally severed us from the law and freed us to marry Him, here and now.

This freedom does not usually come all at once, because our realization of being dead with Christ and raised to new life with Him is something that most of us grow into slowly over many years, as we pursue God. But the provision is already there—we just need to lay hold of it. May God speed us on that journey.

Christ came to destroy the works of the devil (1 John 3:8). He came to free us from past hurts, from our own sin nature, and from legalism. But He did not come to destroy the law; He makes that very clear: "I came not to destroy but to fulfill" (Matthew 5:17). His fulfillment of the law is two-fold: He fulfills its demand for justice, serving the sentence for our "crimes," paying the penalty for our short-comings by His own death; and He fulfills its standard of righteousness *in us*, as we abide *in Him*, enabling us by His indwelling Spirit to obey what we could not do in our own strength.

As we are raised to new life by Christ's resurrection, He becomes our Bridegroom, with whom we will "bring forth fruit unto God." Here I get a picture of God as the proud Grandpa, beaming with pleasure at the offspring of His Son's marriage.

One kind of "fruit" is in the realm of our character, as in the "fruit of the Spirit" (Galatians 5:22): love, joy, peace, long-suffering (patience), gentleness, goodness, faith, meekness (being teachable), and temperance (self-control). Another kind of fruit is our impact on people around us—people coming to know the truth: new children for the kingdom of God. Both kinds of fruit are born spontaneously as a result of our intimate union with Christ. Both are evidence of life and will lead us toward more life.

In a discussion with my husband, Greg, on this subject— this metaphor of being married first to the law and then to Christ, he made a thought-provoking statement: "If we still see God as a law-maker, we have not yet received Christ as Saviour." This is a big bite to chew on, and it is stated in an extreme way. But I believe that Greg is right, because we cannot be married to two husbands at the same time. God frowns on bigamy!

Marriage endures only "until death do us part." If we really understand and embrace the fact that we were crucified with Christ and are therefore dead to the law, then the obligation and bondage that we had to our first spouse is ended and we have only a wonderful new life with a loving, self-sacrificing husband. Our righteous behaviour then is no longer an effort to earn right-standing with God but a spontaneous and joyous expression of our love for Him, in response to His love for us. Beautiful "children": the offspring of a happy marriage.

If, however, we still find ourselves struggling to do right and straining not to do wrong, always comparing ourselves with others, trying to measure up but forever falling short, we are still in bondage to our dead spouse.

Greg told me that a Christian brother recently shared with him this confession: "Everything I do is motivated by guilt."

The really sad thing is that, among "Christians," this is probably more the rule than the exception. This is as tragic as if Beulah, once happily married and settled in the palace, were to come under a scourge of nightmares about her deceased husband, which then were to throw a pallor of fear and shame and regret on all her waking hours.

Christ Slays the Real Villain

Jehonathan's violent rage at Beulah's husband is a picture of Christ's vengeance toward the enemy of our souls. As God foretold in the Garden of Eden, when He rebuked the serpent, "It [the woman's seed, i.e., Jesus] shall bruise thy head, and thou shalt bruise his heel" (Genesis 3:15, KJV).

I think here of a scene in the movie *The Passion of the Christ*, in the Garden of Gethsemane. This is where Jesus really laid down His life: "Father, if thou be willing, remove this cup from me: nevertheless not my will, but thine, be done" (Luke 22:42). The crucifixion the next day was just the playing-out of His decision, His commitment, His self-sacrifice. It was in that second Garden that the stage was set, the deed was done, the battle was fought, and the war was won.

In *The Passion*, as we watch Jesus wrestling with his flesh—his own will, and as we see the snake slithering here and there in the half-light, the scene culminates in a startling and dramatic and symbolic move: Jesus, now fully submitted to the Father and full of resolve, rises to his feet and suddenly, violently, smashes his heel down on the serpent's head.

And so Prince Jehonathan, having run the villain through with his sword, crushes his head beneath his heel.

Father, Son, and Holy Spirit

The king, of course, is a picture of God, whose righteous rule is an alloy forged of both justice and love. His only begotten Son has His Father's eyes: He is "full of grace and truth" (John 1:14). He is the perfect expression of the nature of God: the embodiment of both the "hard" things—righteousness, justice, and truth—and the "soft" things—mercy, love, and grace.

Kletos, tutor, confidante, comforter, and advisor, is, as the reader may have guessed, a type of the Holy Spirit. I took the name from the Greek for Comforter, *parakletos*, (as the Holy Spirit is called in John 14:16, 26). Kletos is sent in the interest of the king and his son wherever they, for now, cannot go.

The kingdom is called Owr because this is the Hebrew word for *light*. God has "delivered us from the power of darkness" and has "translated us into the kingdom of his dear Son" (Col. 1:13). Jesus is the Prince of the Kingdom of Light.

Jehonathan means "given by God." The handsome prince may have seemed, to the fine and flirtatious young ladies of the court, to be God's gift to women, but Jesus was literally God's gift to all of mankind. Jesus, like Jehonathan, is altogether approachable: whether to a person of high or low estate, it makes no difference, for He "is no respecter of persons" (Acts 10:34; see also James 2:1-9). "The one who comes to Me I will most certainly not cast out [I will never, no, never reject one of them who comes to Me]" (John 6:37, AMPC). Until we do come to Him, He loves us from a distance, again like Jehonathan, sending protection, provision, and blessing, however oblivious we remain of the Source.

The quote upon which Jehonathan muses as he rides in the parade is from 2 Samuel 23:4, KJV. It is actually King David speaking, as the Spirit of God speaks through him (according to verse 2). I believe that this is a prophetic utterance, looking ahead to the future reign of Christ here on earth. Listen to how the NIV translates it: "When one rules over men in righteousness, when he rules in the fear of God, he is like the light of morning at sunrise on a cloudless morning, like the brightness after rain that brings the grass from the earth."

I love this scripture! Mornings like that, when I walk outside and everything is so clear and fresh and full of hope and promise, I remember this quote and I think to myself, *Somehow, this is what the reign of Jesus is like.* I remember, then, some lines from a poem by Robert Browning, and I speculate once again that he must have felt the same joy.

Morning's at seven;
The hill-side's dew-pearled; ...
God's in his heaven—
All's right with the world!

Nancy Fowler Christenson

The Sheep and the Shepherd

Although the sheep play only a minor role in the story, they remind us of a few important truths. They know their shepherd's voice by now, and they follow him obediently. Do we? John 10 tells us that the sheep won't listen to a stranger—or a hired hand, who only has his own interests at heart. The employee's motivation is strictly self-preservation. Do we listen to the voices of these hirelings: Fear, Self-Pity, Anger, Bitterness, Common Sense? If we do, they'll lead us down the garden path. We must listen only to the true Shepherd.

When the enemy happens upon you in his prowling (1 Peter 5:8), catches you and mauls you, do you allow him to drag you away from the flock where he can finish you off? "Let us not give up meeting together…but let us encourage one another" (Hebrews 10:25, NIV). Do you know that the Shepherd has servants in His Church who will help you drive away the enemy and then doctor you skilfully? Do you know that no matter what terrible shape we are in when He finds us, He still knows that we can be saved? Do you know that when you are injured or weak or vulnerable, He will (cf. Isaiah 40:11) carry you in His bosom, close to His heart?

The Blood of the Lamb

I have brought the Blood of the Lamb into the story in a roundabout way: it has soiled the cloak that the prince-in-disguise wraps around Beulah's shoulders. Jehonathan expects her to recoil from the ugly stain, but she sees instead something very beautiful. The lamb's blood on the garment convinces Beulah of the character of her young man: she sees that he has a selfless heart of love and compassion.

How much more does the Lamb's blood convince us of God's love? "God shows his love for us in that while we were yet sinners Christ died for us" (Romans 5:8, RSV). There are some so-called Christians who recoil at the mention of the Blood of Jesus, thinking it gory and distasteful and unnecessary. If only they could perceive how necessary it was that God's Son shed His Blood! Gory and distasteful as the Crucifixion was, it would become, to all who have eyes to see, an unspeakably beautiful demonstration of love. And it is the Blood that overcomes our arch-enemy (Revelation 12:11).

Jehonathan's cloak symbolizes a covering for Beulah's tainted past. "Love covers over a multitude of sins" (1 Peter 4:8, NIV). "I will greatly rejoice in the Lord, my soul shall be joyful in my God; for he hath clothed me with the garments of salvation, he hath covered me with the robe of righteousness, as a bridegroom decketh himself with ornaments, and as a bride adorneth herself with her jewels" (Isaiah 61:10, KJV).

Ironically, the Blood of Jesus doesn't soil or stain: it makes clean. "They…have washed their robes, and made them white in the blood of the Lamb" (Revelation 7:14, KJV).

There is another mention in scripture of a robe dipped in blood; it's in a picture of our Heavenly Prince, coming for us on—how fitting!—a white steed. "And I saw heaven opened, and behold a white horse; and he that sat upon him was called Faithful and True, and in righteousness he doth judge and make war. His eyes were as a flame of fire, and on his head were many crowns; and he had a name written, that no man knew, but he himself. And he was clothed with a vesture dipped in blood: and his name is called The Word of God" (Revelation 19:11-13, KJV).

The Gift of Purity

To me, the most important symbol in the story is in something the prince says to his bride-to-be in one of their final exchanges: "I love you," he says. "Let that be your virtue."

I have long since learned—yet I am learning more every day—that God loves me, with an everlasting love, in the person of His Son. I've learned that this is my only real virtue, and that it is more than enough. This is my imputed righteousness, not a righteousness earned, but received as a gift, bought by the death of Christ. Jesus became sin for me that I might be, in Him, the righteousness of God (cf. 2 Corinthians 5:21). This is my purity—not fleeting innocence, but pure gold that endures, through a fiery furnace, as God purges me. And as He does His purifying work in me, slowly working out in my life the righteousness that He put in when I first embraced Him, He has never once asked that I come up sinless, only that I be found faithful—full of faith. It is by our faith that we please God (cf. Hebrews 11:6), because this is the "good works" that God desires of us: simply that we believe on the One Whom He has sent (cf. John 6:28, 29; 1 John 3:22-23).

A God of Passion

Prince Jehonathan first meets the maid in the spring, when "the winter is past and the rains are over and gone." This quote is directly from the Song of Solomon (2:11-12). It always speaks to me of spring as a time for new love, when the long, barren winter of loneliness is over. It's when the Lover calls the Beloved to come away with Him. Some readers will have recognized other bits of dialogue from the "Song of Songs": "You have stolen my heart with one glance of your eyes" (4:9,

NIV). "My beloved is mine and I am his" (2:16, KJV). "Oh, let me see your form, let me hear your voice; for your voice is sweet, and your form is lovely" (2:14, NASB).

Do we dare to believe that God extends Himself to us in such intimate terms, that He desires this kind of exchange with us, this kind of relationship? I think that, like Jehonathan, He longs to be loved simply for Who He Is, neither submitted to in craven fear nor courted selfishly for what He can give us. He is a passionate God who longs for us to know Him the way He knows us. He wants to share His passion with us.

The Prince cuts a dashing figure, leaving in his wake sighing, swooning women. When Jesus walked on earth, however, there was nothing particularly attractive or desirable about His human appearance (Isaiah 53:2). But scripture says elsewhere that He is altogether lovely (Song of Solomon 5:16). This "second opinion" is the perception of the Beloved, who is the symbol of the Bride of Christ. She is the one who really knows Him. Now that we are new creations in Christ, "even though we once did estimate Christ from a human viewpoint and as a man, yet now [we have such knowledge of Him that] we know Him no longer [in terms of the flesh] (2 Corinthians 5:16b, AMPC). We know Jesus by the Spirit, which is the way Jehonathan wants to be known and loved, not for his stature or his countenance but for his heart (1 Sam. 16:7).

"The Spirit and the Bride say Come" (Rev. 22:17)

Jesus, like Jehonathan, is anticipating His wedding. "For this cause shall a man leave his father and mother, and shall be joined unto his wife, and they two shall be one flesh. This is a great mystery: but I speak concerning Christ and the church" (Ephesians 5:31, 32, KJV).

The Father of the Groom is waiting patiently, still holding out, "not wishing for any to perish but for all to come to repentance" (2 Peter 3:9, NASB). Christ is waiting only for His Bride to be fully prepared, her rites of purification completed, "that he might present it to himself a glorious church, not having spot, or wrinkle, or any such thing; but that it should be holy and without blemish" (Ephesians 5:27, KJV). Then He will be able to say, "You are altogether beautiful, my darling, and there is no blemish in you" (Song of Solomon 4:7, NASB).

His Father will tell Him when the time is right. "No one knows about that day or hour, not even the angels in heaven, nor the Son, but only the Father" (Mark 13:32, NIV). Jesus is just waiting for His Father to give the word: "It's time, Son—go and get her."

And then we will all really live happily ever after.

Other Works by the Author

Yes, I Really Was a Cowgirl
The very personal story of a young woman who took a job as a
cow-camp cook on Canada's largest cattle ranch and fell in
love with the cowboy way of life.
A humorous and heartwarming memoir.

Nonfiction/Autobiographical
300 pages/100 photos
Print book only
http://www.cowgirlstory.com
Magazine reviews & readers' comments:
http://www.cowgirlstory.com/reviews.htm

Cookhouse Capers
An audio collection of rollicking, rhythmic poems inspired by
the author's experiences in the book above, interspersed with
music composed by her son Ben.
Inquire at nancy@ogdenfish.com

Made in Heaven, Fleshed Out on Earth
After a passionate but pure courtship, Nancy Fowler
anticipated uninhibited sexual bliss in her marriage to Greg
Christenson. She couldn't have been more surprised and
bewildered when, once the vows were said,
"someone turned off the passion switch."
Believing, however, that every marriage is *Made in Heaven*
and that God is a very present help as His design is *Fleshed
Out on Earth*, they journey on together, choosing to trust that
God will eventually cause them to triumph.

Nonfiction/Autobiography
Print book, 290 pages
Audio book available; ebook coming soon
http://www.madeinheavenbook.com

"Essential to young adults! I wish I had read this in high
school. This is the book you pick up when you are someone
like me—married and having issues in the intimate department
and lost and crying out for help. This is a chronicle of life, of
relationships, of heartbreak, of the pain of ignoring the Lord
and His design for sexual purity and marriage, the journey
back to Him, and the blessings received."
— B.M., age 25

Music Made in Heaven
An audio collection of original songs, written along the
journey of the story above.
Inquire at nancy@ogdenfish.com

Rape and Redemption
Nineteen-year-old Donna is brutally gang-raped.
The next fifteen years are a struggle
between despair and faith:
a long, dark journey back into wholeness.
God shows Himself to be "a very present help in trouble"
(Psalm 46:1, KJV), intervening and orchestrating
miraculously.
A story of tangible hope for those broken
by sexual abuse of any kind,
as told to Nancy Christenson.

Ebook
Print Book
at your favourite online retailer

Author Info & Contact

Nancy Christenson has loved writing for as long as she can remember. She lives near Wetaskiwin, Alberta, Canada, with her husband, Greg. They have four adult children: two sons and two daughters, plus a growing circle of in-laws and grandchildren.

She can be contacted at nancy@ogdenfish.com.

Visit the website:
http://www.ogdenfish.com
Inspirational blog:
http://www.ogdenfish2.blogspot.com

The Prince of Owr and *Rape and Redemption* are both available at cost for women's ministries.
Please inquire.